I Heard My Mother Call My Name

I Heard My Mother Call My Name

by
NANCY HUNDAL

illustrated by
LAURA FERNANDEZ

HarperCollins*Publishers*Ltd

Produced by Caterpillar Press for
HarperCollins Publishers Ltd
Suite 2900, Hazelton Lanes
55 Avenue Road
Toronto, Ontario, Canada M5R 3L2

Text copyright © 1990 by Nancy Hundal
Illustrations copyright © 1990 by Jacobson Fernandez
Photography by Ian Crylser
All rights reserved

Canadian Cataloguing in Publication Data

Hundal, Nancy, 1957-
  I heard my mother call my name

ISBN 0-00-223738-5 (bound)
ISBN 0-00-647496-9 (pbk.)

I. Fernandez, Laura. II. Title.

PS8565.U5635143 1990 jC813'.54 C90-093556-1
PZ7.H85Ih 1990

To Edith Erickson and Margery Ferguson
For my grandmas, with love.
N.H.

For Michael,
who has been the greatest joy in my life,
I dedicate this book. I love you.
L.F.

I heard my mother call my name and I know I should go in, but it is summer and dusk and beautiful. Behind me in the house are soft sounds — quiet voices and a faraway song.

Here on the porch, everything is still. I look out past the trees and into the street. Shapes move dreamily, back and forth. Is something there, or does the fuzzy light paint them in my head?

I heard my mother call my name and I know I should go in . . .

But the fireflies are playing hide and seek in the shadows. There aren't too many places to hide when you carry your own light. They twinkle through the trees, silently chasing each other. Up and up they fly, like tiny fireworks.

I heard my mother call my name and I know I should go in . . .

But the last of my friends are flowing off to their homes, leaving their good-byes floating behind them in the dusky air. The voices seem to linger long after my friends are gone. Do they wash around in the dark all night, waiting for the games to begin again in the buttery morning sun?

I heard my mother call my name and I know I should go in . . .

But a ginger cat has tiptoed up beside me, and rubs her softness against my leg. When I scratch her ears, she begins to purr and meows once — a lonely, lovely meow. Is she sad to see the darkness take the children from the street, or glad for the quiet, cool peace? I look at her carefully, but I can't tell.

I heard my mother call my name and I know I should go in . . .

But the flowers, the night flowers have opened. Their scent explodes softly around me, stealing through the garden and over the lawn. The sweet smell of the grass bubbles up to meet the trails of flower perfume. I take a deep, deep breath.

I heard my mother call my name and I know I should go in . . .

But the sun's fingertips are reaching their final grasp across the sky. The moon's calm smile glows behind the trees. I look at the tiny pool of silver around the moon, and at the great river of orange near the sun. Are they looking at me?

I heard my mother call my name and I know I should go in . . .

But there's a squeak, squeak, squeak coming from across the street. A mouse? I don't think so. I peer across, and see a steady, gentle movement back and forth. Must be Mrs. Bell on her porch, rocking and watching in the dark. Back and forth, rocking and watching.

The heat of the day slips away with the sun. A cool breeze licks my face and hair. It feels good. The street seems so calm and cool that it's hard to imagine it an hour ago — hot, jumpy, noisy. I try to picture it in the middle of the night, then covered in falling leaves, buried in snow. Suddenly, it seems very cool.

I heard my mother call my name and I know I should go in . . .

But I hear a busy, buzzy noise near the sidewalk. What's out there? Only a couple of toy cars forgotten from a game. Are they revving their engines, impatient for me to disappear so they can race the night away? The street lamp begins to glow, growing brighter and brighter, until I can see the cars easily. Still the buzzing. I look up to the lamp and see a swarm of tiny flies, crashing and diving towards the light. Buzzing.

I heard my mother call my name and I know I should go in . . .

But two people are strolling past my gate, hand in hand. They are speaking very quietly. They don't see me. Down the street, I hear a baby cry, then a window shut. Quiet again.

The ticking machine of the street slows to the soft hum of night. The air is like velvet.

I hear my mother call my name . . .

Time to go in.